To Brooks, Donna, Dana, Nellie, and all of Team Otter!
(Except for Giraffe.)

Balzer + Bray is an imprint of HarperCollins Publishers.
Otter Loves Easter!
Copyright © 2017 by Sam Garton

Library of Congress Control Number: 2016935873
ISBN 978-0-06-236667-2

The artist used Adobe Photoshop to create the digital illustrations for this book.
Typography by Kathleen Duncan
17 18 19 20   PC   10 9 8 7 6 5 4 3 2
❖
First Edition

OTTER

Loves Easter!

SAM GARTON

BALZER + BRAY
An Imprint of HarperCollinsPublishers

It was Easter morning.
Teddy and I were very excited!

The Easter Bunny had brought
me lots of chocolate eggs.
I love the Easter Bunny!
There were:

1 bag of
small eggs

1 bag of jelly
beans

4 medium-size
eggs

1 pair of bunny ears

3 big eggs

12 small eggs in a basket

1 gold bunny

After counting all my goodies carefully,
I went to tell Otter Keeper the news.

But then I wished I hadn't,
because he said I had to share my
eggs with my friends.

What a ridiculous idea! I couldn't share
my eggs. They were mine!

I tried to give one of my eggs to Giraffe, but I had to take it back because it didn't belong to Giraffe. It was mine.

I decided I would have to try harder.

But sharing is very hard.
Because eating chocolate is very easy.

When Otter Keeper called us for
breakfast, there was a problem.

Nobody was hungry. I also felt a little sick.

So instead of eating breakfast, I took a nap.

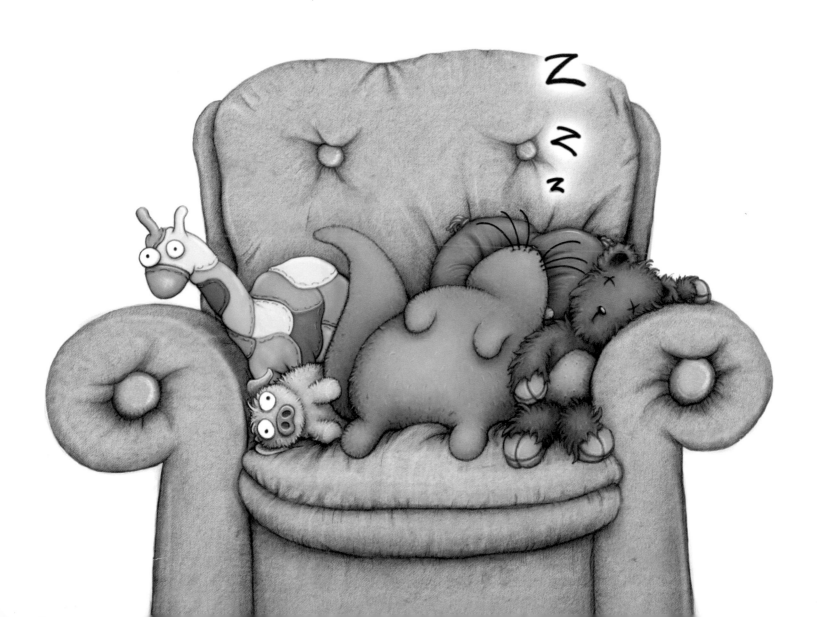

When I woke up I felt a lot better, but there was a new problem:
All the Easter eggs were in my tummy, and my friends hadn't gotten any.

We needed someone to save Easter!

Someone who had fluffy bunny ears and a fluffy tail.
Someone who was really good at sharing. We needed . . .

the Easter Otter!

There was lots of work to do.

It was lucky that the Easter Otter
was an Easter expert.

Otter Keeper helped a little too, because even an Easter expert needs help from a grown-up sometimes.

Finally, the surprise was ready!

It was the best Easter egg hunt ever!

Pig found an egg
buried in the sandbox.

Teddy found an egg
under the bucket.

It took him a while, but Giraffe found an egg in the end too.

There was even an egg for Otter Keeper!

My friends were so happy to have eggs of their own,
and we all agreed that sharing is very important.

Giraffe said the Easter Otter was a hero, and Giraffe was right. I had saved Easter!

And then, to say thank you, my friends did something very kind.

They decided to share their eggs with me.